This book belongs to:
MW00874479

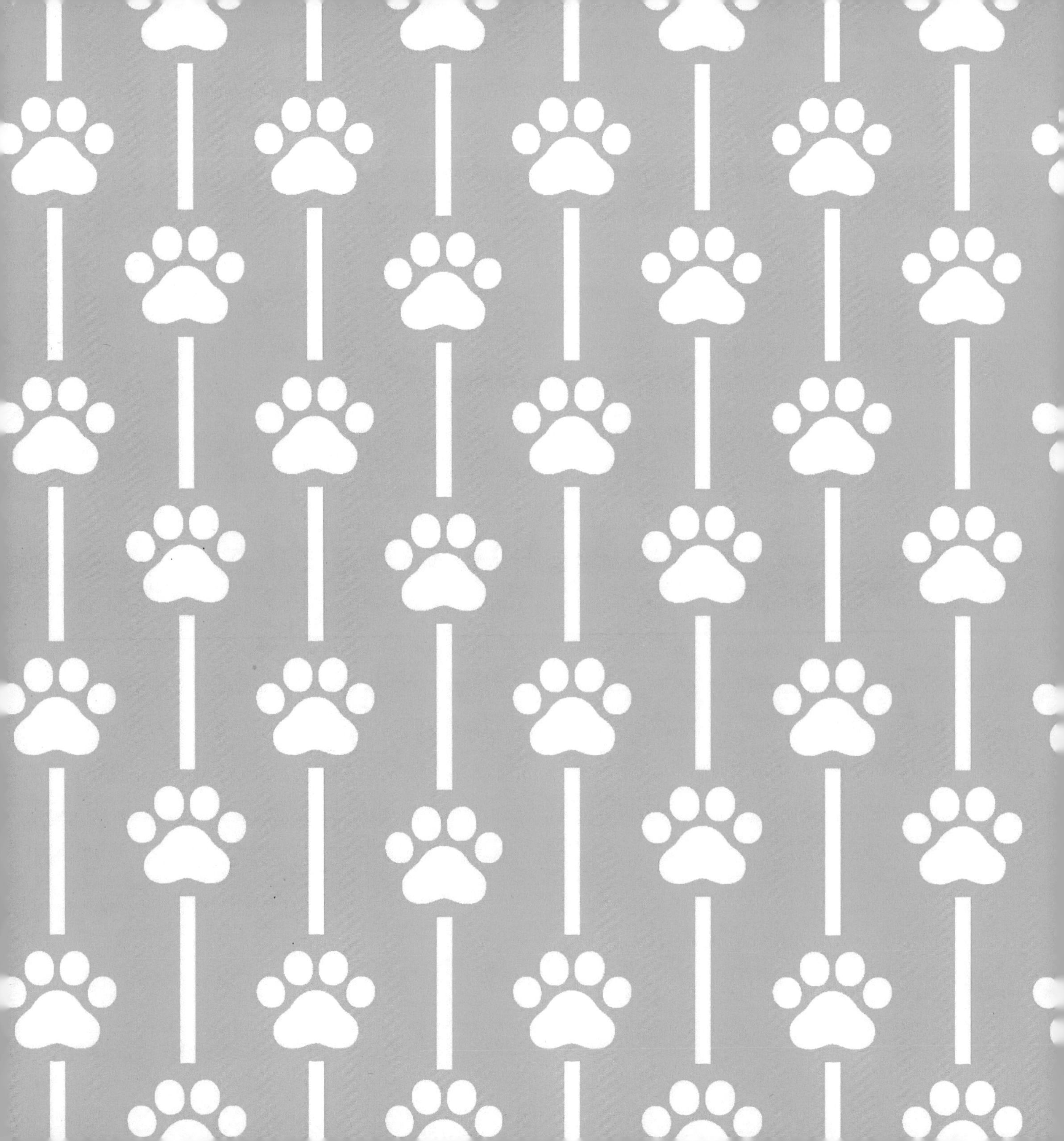

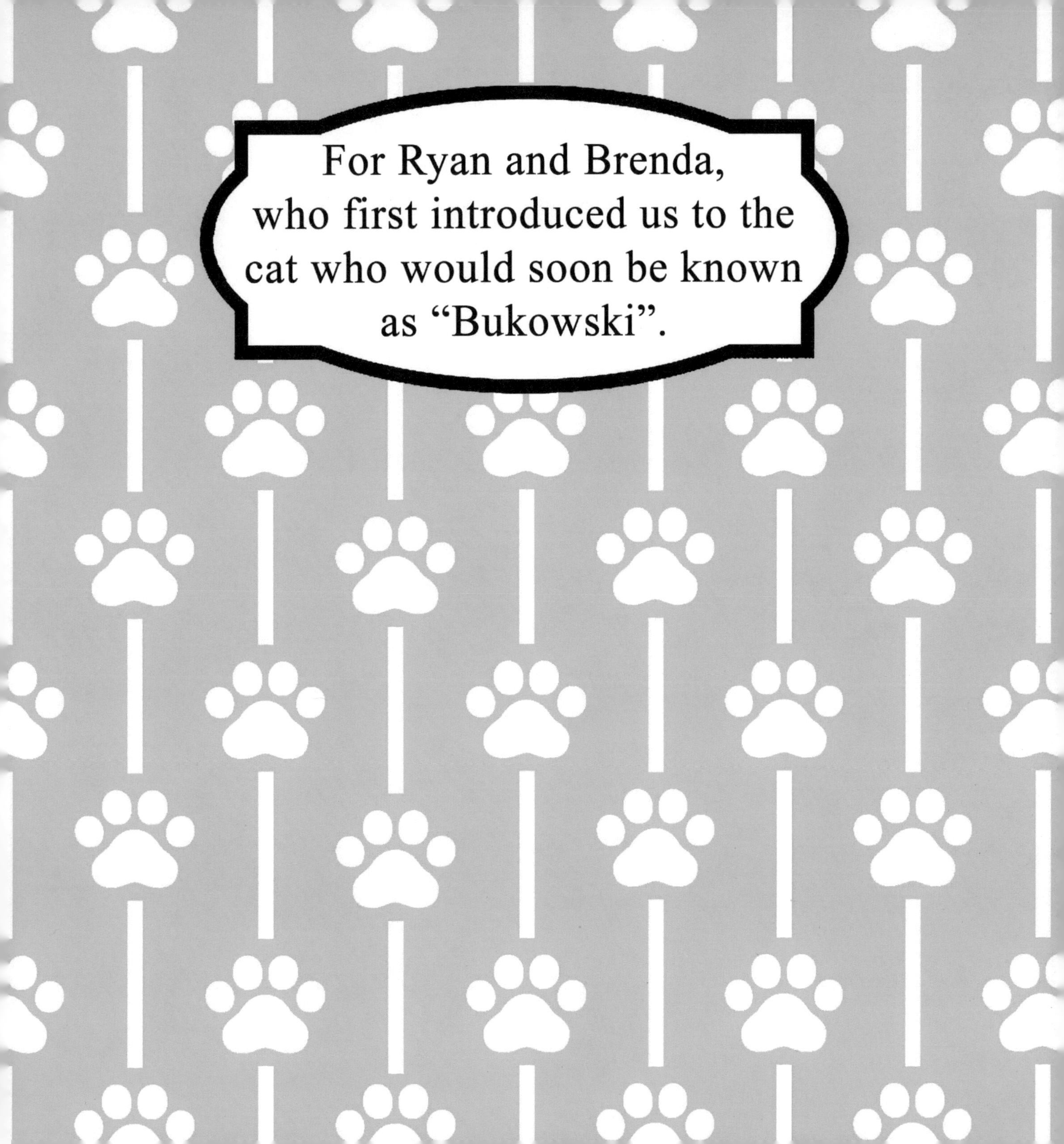
For Ryan and Brenda,
who first introduced us to the
cat who would soon be known
as “Bukowski”.

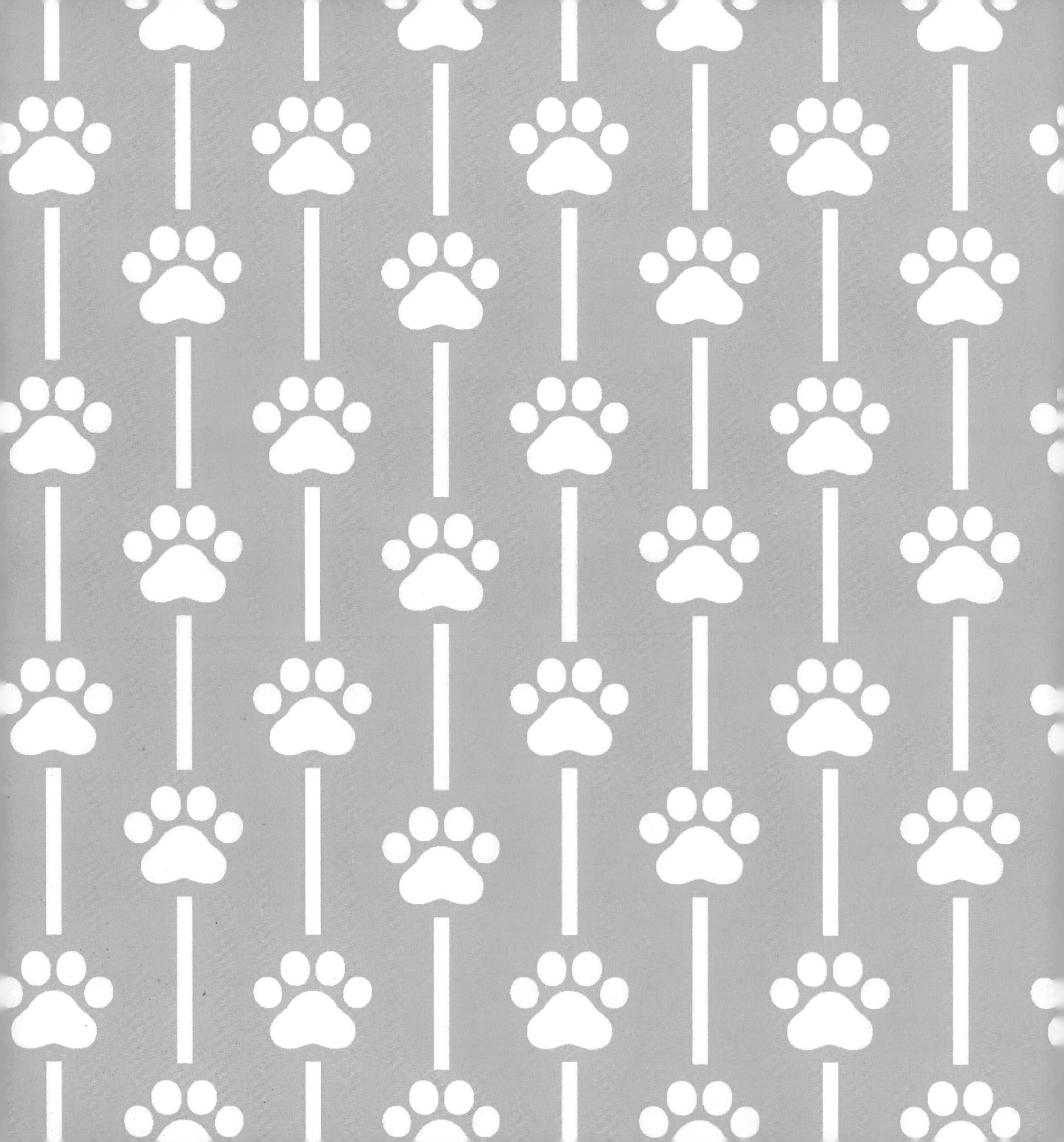

The Many Adventures Of BUKOWSKI THE CAT

Book #1: "The Royal Introduction"

written & illustrated by

Chris Brady

A portion of the proceeds from your purchase of this book will go directly to *Harrison's Halfway House* Cat & Kitten Foster and Rescue Sanctuary, helping Philadelphia's wayward cats find their forever homes.

This book was printed in the United States of America, at BookBaby, 7905 N. Crescent Blvd., Pennsauken, NJ 08110

Published by BradyRain Media, 2020

Hello there! My name is Bukowski,
And I'm the best cat in the world.
At least that's what my Daddy tells me
When he says that I'm his special girl.
But I'm in no position to doubt him,
Or question what makes me so great
When he wants to say I am his princess
And put yummy food on my plate!

Mommy says I am just spoiled,
And she loves me, but Daddy is nuts
Because he is always kissing me,
Singing, or making a fuss.

Nowadays I'm a confident kitty,
With the mindset of a great queen.
But I used to be so scared and nervous,
I hid behind the washing machine!

It's true! When I first came to live here,
I wasn't too friendly or kind.
The washing machine in the laundry room
Was the perfect place for me to hide!

Daddy would sit and be patient.
He'd play his guitar and sing songs.
He'd make up ones about me, him, and Mommy
To help me get comfy and strong.

Mommy talked to me through the washer
Before she even saw my face.
She wanted me to get used to her voice,
And it helped me feel calm and feel safe.

The two of them must have looked crazy,
And I giggle now when I think of
Them singing and talking to the washing machine,
But that's how I knew I was loved.

So I came out from behind my hiding spot,
And greeted them both with a...
MEOW!
Letting them know I was finally ready
To be their sweet kitty cat now.

Once I met Mom and Dad, I knew right away
That I was meant to be here.

They know that I love to have my belly rubbed,
And they scratch that itch on my ear!

They feed me, and pet me, we have “lazy time”,
And watch movies with me on their lap...

We chase around lasers...
And bat at string toys...

sneakers
SALE
BUKOWSKI

And there's tons of good places to nap!

Even after they come home at night,
And are tired from “work”, like they say,
Mommy and Daddy always find time
To include me into their day.

They are never too busy to give me
All of their love and affection.
Sometimes I'm even nice enough
To give them some of my attention!

A lot's changed since I first came to live here.
Some new pets have joined our family.
And it's always my job to keep them in line,
Play with them, and help them eat treats.

I guess the moral of my little story,
And the point that I'm trying to make,
Is, Mommies and Daddies, and children, too,
Be patient, for goodness sake!

Not all cats will be playful like doggies.
Most of us aren't, I'm sure!
We won't run around, or do tricks for you,
We won't beg, and you might be ignored.

Kitties are different, we have our own speed,
We get sleepy, we're moody, we hiss.
We'll scratch and we'll claw if you play too rough,
I'm warning you about this!

But give us some time to get used to you,
And take time to get to know us, too.
And sooner or later, when we want to show love,
We'll give you a headbutt or two.

And kitties please listen - this part is important!
This advice needs to be known!
Don't spend all of your time hiding from
The nice people who gave you a home!

It’s okay to be nervous and scared at first,
But try to keep an open mind.
Most people who welcome cats into their homes
Are loving, and patient, and kind.

And one thing I've learned from my Mom and Dad,
Is that true love was meant to be shared.
Thinking back now to the day I first met them,
I can't believe I was so scared!

I’m happy, and chubby, well-fed, and admired,
I’m cuddled, and spoiled, and clean...

All because I took a chance and came out
From behind the washing machine!

Hers
His
The End.

The Story Behind the Story

When my teaching career ended, I knew that I wanted to continue working with children, but I wasn't sure how or in what capacity. I am a songwriter, and I am always writing and singing little jingles to and about my cats. One day, the idea came to me to combine the two, and write and record a children's album about my cats. Over time, that idea evolved from an album full of cat-centric songs to a series of children's books about cats.

Anna and I love to reminisce about the early days of Bukowski (our first cat and resident cat princess) coming to live with us. We laugh about her quirks and gush about how much she has grown over the years. Suddenly, it hit me, and my book series had its star.

I did not want to simply create a "Cat Calls The Shots" story and become a blatant ripoff of the beloved Garfield comics because A- I can not and would never dream of comparing myself to the legendary works of the genius Jim Davis, and B- I really wanted to write in a way that I personally haven't seen before.

The teacher in me took over and decided that these books would be told by the point of view of Bukowski, but that in each story, not only would she be talking to other cats (and children), but she would also inevitably learn a valuable lesson or offer some valuable advice to other cats, cat owners, and hopefully, the reader.

I wanted to make these stories and the lessons learned within them two-fold, one that cats and cat owners can learn, but ones that are simultaneously relatable to things children deal with on a regular basis.

Our first story introduces us to a shy and nervous girl who needs time to warm up to new surroundings, and how rewarding it can be for cat, owner, child, and reader (!) when trust and love are given the time and space they need to naturally bloom.

Enjoy!

★BUKOWSKI★
Follow Our Real Life Adventures!
@mycatbukowski
@harrisonshalfwayhouse
@bradyrain_media

About The Authors

Bukowski the Cat is the star and narrator of this book. She lives in a cozy little home with her Mommy and Daddy, her kitty sisters, Harley, Quinn, and Jovi, and her dog brother, Benny. She is known to have the special ability to make her parents laugh and can always cheer them up after a bad day. She loves crinkle mats, toys that make her work for treats, watching the cartoon Doc McStuffins, and whatever "people food" Daddy sneaks her when Mommy isn't looking.

Chris and Anna Brady (aka "Mommy and Daddy") live in Philadelphia, PA, and when they aren't busy working at their boring "real jobs", they are home with their four cats and their Jackhuahua. They are the owners and operators of "Harrison's Halfway House" Foster and Rescue Sanctuary for local cats and kittens. Since beginning in the summer of 2016, they have successfully fostered and helped find forever homes for four cats and one pit bull! (And currently have two bonded brothers looking for a new home as this is being written.) They enjoy loud music, horror movies, and rooting for the Flyers.

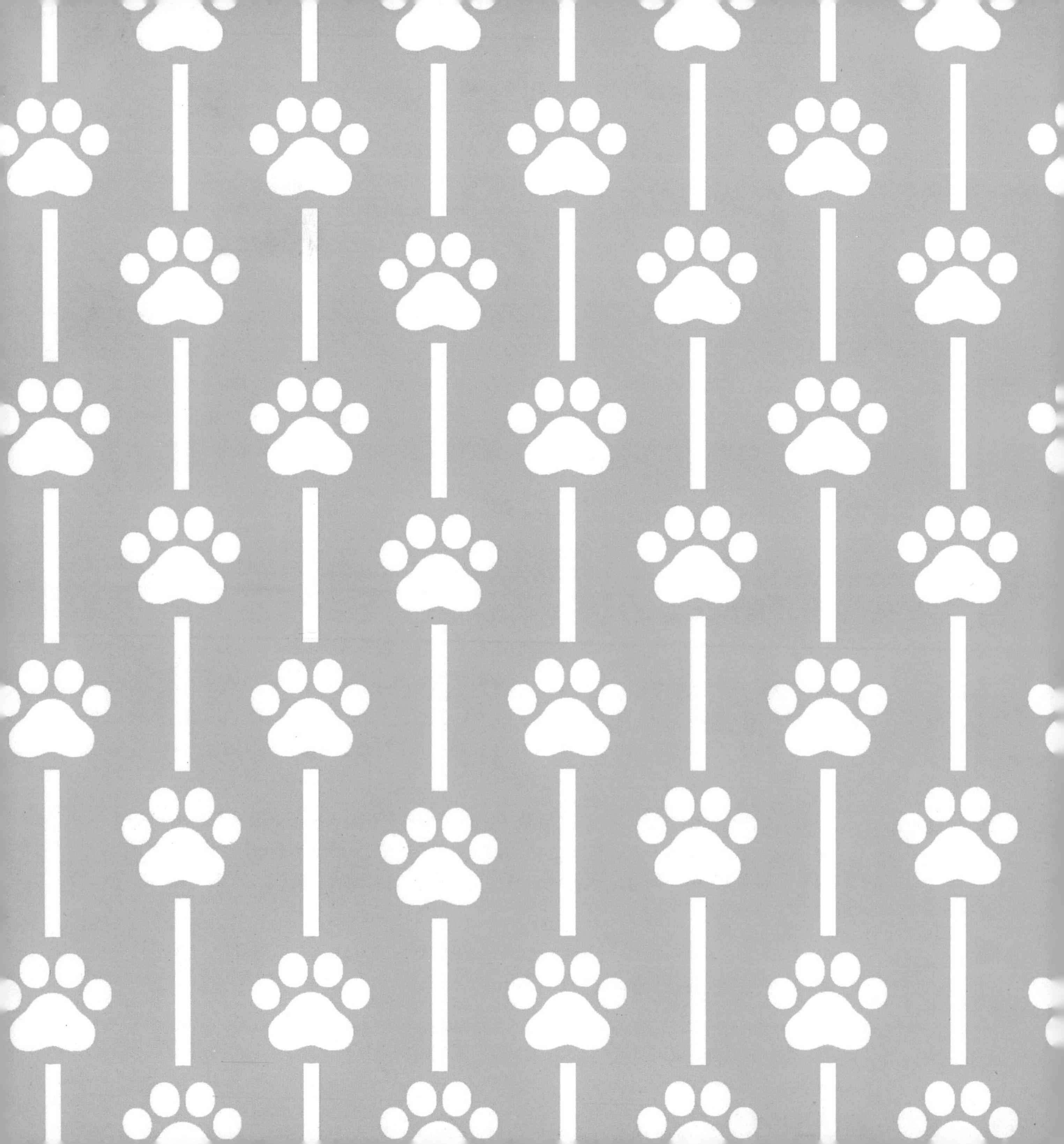